BOOK 4

NANCY CLANCY

Secret of the Silver Key

WRITTEN BY
Jane O'Connor

ILLUSTRATIONS BY
Robin Preiss Glasser

HARPER
An Imprint of HarperCollinsPublishers

Library of Congress Control Number: 2013958341
ISBN 978-0-06-208299-2

Typography by Jeanne L. Hogle
14 15 16 17 18   CG/RRDH   10 9 8 7 6 5 4 3 2
❖
First Edition

For the Handler, who is key in all things!

—J.O'C.

For my childhood pal, Wendy Frontiero

—R.P.G.

CONTENTS

CHAPTER **1**

PAST, PRESENT, FUTURE

"**T**hat's really a camera?" Lionel asked. Nancy could see the skeptical look on his face. "Skeptical" was a new favorite word of hers. It meant a person doubted whether something was true.

"Yup, it belonged to my mom," Mr. Dudeny said. "Fifty years ago, Polaroid

1

cameras like this one were high-tech. They let people take photos in a brand-new way." Nancy's teacher was holding up a silver and black box so everyone in room 3D could see it. The front of the camera pulled out like an accordion with a large, round lens on the end.

"You put in film, snapped a picture, and out popped a piece of paper. In about a minute you'd see the picture appear on it."

"Ooh! It sounds like magic," Clara said. "Can you show how it works?"

"Unfortunately, no. The kind of film you need is hard to find and pretty expensive now. But I have some Polaroid pictures taken with this camera."

Mr. D passed around a bunch of small, square photos. The colors in all of them

were very faded. "My mother is the girl in the tie-dye T-shirt."

"Mr. D, your mom and her friends were hippies!" Nancy said. She and Bree were looking at a photo of a boy with hair down to his shoulders and another of two girls with their arms around each other, one in a floppy hat and blue granny glasses and the other wearing lots of love beads and a necklace with a peace sign.

Grace sat, twirling her pencil and looking bored. "I don't see what's so great. Now you can take photos with a phone and see them in a second. You don't even need a camera."

"Well, Grace, that's the point I'm about to make. A long time ago, this camera was brand-new and cool. Now it's something from the past." Mr. Dudeny took out his cell phone from his pocket. "I bet fifty years from now third graders will look at this and say, 'That thing is really a phone?'"

Nancy mulled over Mr. D's words, which meant she was thinking about them really hard. Once the past hadn't been the past. It had been just like this very moment, sitting in her classroom. The present. And in the future, this very moment would turn into the past. Nancy blinked and shook her head. All this mulling was making her brain feel twisted up like a pretzel.

"Next week, I would like each of you to bring in something from present time.

Nothing big. Something that tells about what life is like today—like a desk calendar for this year or the front page of a newspaper. We are going to put everything in a box."

"You mean, like, a time capsule?" Lionel said. "Awesome!"

"Ooh—and can it have a sign on the front that says 'Do not open until 2064'?" Nancy asked.

Mr. D nodded and explained that their time capsule would be stored in the basement.

"Maybe in fifty years my child will go to school here and get to open it," Clara said.

Grace rolled her eyes. "Clara. Do the math. In fifty years you'll be nearly sixty. Your children won't be kids anymore.

They'll be grown-ups too."

Clara pooched out her lips and looked disappointed. "Oh yeah, you're right." Then she brightened. "Well . . . then maybe my grandchildren will get to open it." Clara giggled. "Imagine! Me, a grandma!"

"And for Monday," Mr. Dudeny went on, "I'd like each of you to interview somebody who was your age a long time ago. Thirty, forty, or even fifty years ago. Find out where they grew up and what it was like being a kid back then. What was happening in the world? Who was president? Were there exciting new inventions? Any crazy fads?"

Bree was furiously scribbling down everything Mr. D said. Then she turned and whispered to Nancy, "Dibs on Mrs. DeVine."

"No fair!" Nancy whispered back. Mrs.

DeVine was their neighbor and also a senior citizen. She was the perfect person to interview, and Nancy had just as much right to pick Mrs. DeVine as Bree did.

Nancy raised her hand and waved it around it until she got her teacher's attention. "Mr. D, Mr. D! What if two people want to interview the same person?"

Mr. D said that wasn't a problem.

"Let's do the interview together. It'll be way more fun that way," Nancy suggested right after the last bell rang.

"Okay. Sure!" Then suddenly Bree looked uncertain. "Hmmmm. Maybe that's not allowed." Bree was always very particular about following homework rules. So before heading outside to where their bikes were parked, they got the okay from their teacher.

By the time they biked home, a plan was in place. In the clubhouse in Nancy's backyard, they made a beautiful invitation to slip under Mrs. DeVine's door.

Nancy Clancy and Bree James request the pleasure of your company on Saturday at four o'clock at their clubhouse.
Refreshments will be served.

P.S. We would like to ask you about the olden days when you were a child.

"It's so weird to think Mrs. DeVine was our age once," Bree said, placing the cap back on a hot-pink marker.

"Everything about time is weird when you really start thinking about it," Nancy said. She sat back on her knees and pondered. "Right now, Monday is the future. And by Monday, today will already be the past. Doesn't it make your brain feel twisted up like a pretzel?"

Bree thought for a moment. Then she giggled and said, "No. More like scrambled eggs!"

CHAPTER 2

THE INTERVIEW

Bree James: Thank you very much, Mrs. DeVine, for agreeing to this interview. We will now begin. My first question for you is: Who was the president of the United States when you were born?

Mrs. DeVine: It was Harry Truman. He became president at the very end of World War II in 1945. That was the year I

11

was born. Actually, he liked to be known as Harry S. Truman. Although he didn't have a middle name, he picked a middle initial for himself. I guess he thought it made him sound more important, more distinguished.

Nancy Clancy: Where were you born? Was it in this country or were you an immigrant?

Mrs. DeVine: Why, I was born right in this very town! Only, it wasn't much of a town then. There was still lots of farmland.

Bree James: Were there any amazing new inventions like the Polaroid camera?

Mrs. DeVine: Oh, yes! TV. Television screens were tiny at first, and you needed antennas—"rabbit ears," we called them— to keep the picture in focus. And the shows were all in black-and-white.

Nancy Clancy: What were your favorites?

Mrs. DeVine: That's easy: *I Love Lucy.* I'd go over to my best friend's house to watch, because her family had a TV set long before mine did. Lucy was a grown woman, but she and her friend Ethel would get themselves into the craziest trouble! My best friend and I were jealous because nothing crazy ever happened to us.

Nancy Clancy: Who was your best friend?

Mrs. DeVine: Her name was Bitsy. But she wasn't little. In fact she was very tall for her age. Bitsy was a nickname for Elizabeth.

Bree James: Since Nancy asked two

questions in a row, I get to ask two now. What did you do for fun? I mean, besides watching TV? And were there any fads?

Mrs. DeVine: Oh, we did a lot of same things you girls like to do. We rode our bikes, we played board games like Monopoly and Sorry! And we read all of the Nancy Drew books.

Bree James: What about fads?

Mrs. DeVine: Bitsy and I loved jacks. I was very good. I could do lots of tricks, which were called "fancies" and had names like Snake in the Grass and Backsies. Slinkys were very popular too. Bitsy and I would have races to see whose Slinky would tumble downstairs the fastest.

Nancy Clancy: What kind of clothes did you wear?

Mrs. DeVine: Girls wore skirts most of the time. Poodle skirts were the rage. And if we wore pants, they weren't blue jeans. Blues were for boys and were called "dungarees." I brought over an old photo album so you can see what kids looked like in the 1950s.

Nancy Clancy: This brings our interview to a close. Thank you, Mrs. DeVine. Your answers have told us many interesting things about the days of yore.

CHAPTER 3

A LONG-LOST FRIEND

"**D**oes Bitsy live close by now? Do you still see each other all the time?" Nancy asked before biting into a Nilla wafer cookie. Now with the interview over, refreshments were being served in the clubhouse.

Mrs. DeVine shook her head. "I'm afraid

we lost touch ages ago. Her family moved when we were about twelve. We tried staying in touch, but once we weren't neighbors or going to the same school, well"—Mrs. DeVine shrugged her shoulders—"it just wasn't the same."

Bree was drinking pink lemonade out of a teacup. She gulped and sputtered, "That's so terrible. To lose your best friend!"

Nancy felt the exact same way.

"We didn't have a falling-out or anything. We just drifted apart. Bitsy had new friends. So did I. We didn't have much in common anymore."

"When was the last time you saw each other?" Nancy asked.

"Why, it was so long ago, I don't even

remember." Mrs. DeVine pursed her lips, which were Passionately Red. That was the name of the lipstick she always wore. "Oh, I do know. We bumped into each other at a clothing store. We both had our eyes on the same prom dress. So that had to be . . ." Mrs. DeVine paused and started ticking off years on her fingers. Her long fingernails were Passionately Red too. "Well, I can't believe it, but it must have been nearly fifty years ago!"

Nancy and Bree exchanged identical looks. They were way more than surprised. They were stupefied. "But you were best friends. And—and you both liked the same exact dress. That proves you still had stuff in common," Nancy said. The longest she and Bree had gone without seeing each other was four weeks last summer, when both their families took two-week vacations and the weeks didn't overlap. Even with email and phone calls, it had seemed like forever. An eternity.

"Bitsy was a wonderful girl. I remember her with great fondness," Mrs. DeVine went on. "There's a special closeness with your first best friend. Now, scoot a little closer. I'm sure there are pictures of Bitsy in here." Mrs. DeVine opened the red spiral-bound album that she'd brought over.

"That's yours truly!" Mrs. DeVine laughed, pointing to a photo of a girl on a swing.

"No way!" Bree cried. "I never would have guessed."

Nancy wouldn't have either. It was hard

to imagine the girl in the photo who had dark braids and wore eyeglasses turning into their glamorous neighbor with her platinum-blond hair and false eyelashes.

"There. That's Bitsy with me at a county fair."

In the photo, Bitsy stood half a head taller than Mrs. DeVine, only she wasn't Mrs. DeVine back then, Nancy realized. She was called Margie, which was short for Marjorie. The girls had their arms around each other and, in their free hands, they held paper cones of cotton candy. Their mouths were wide-open, as if they'd just heard the punch line to a really funny joke.

Although the photo showed two happy friends, it made Nancy sad to look at it. And what did Mrs. DeVine mean about having a "first best friend"? A best friend was forever. Nancy looked over at Bree, who was turning the pages of the album. Sure, sometimes they got into fights, but they loved each other.

"Mrs. DeVine, what if Nancy and I tried tracking Bitsy down for you? Imagine seeing each other after all these years."

Yes! Finding a missing person! How thrilling that would be. "We have excellent sleuthing skills," Nancy added. "We figured out who stole something valuable from our classroom, and we did it by cleverly following clues." Nancy hoped that didn't sound like she was bragging. But she and Bree were sharp detectives. The only problem was that there hadn't been any crimes lately. Finding a missing person wasn't like a robbery. Still, it was mysterious.

It was obvious, however, that Mrs. DeVine didn't take their offer seriously. "Oh no. I wouldn't know where to tell you to start looking. Bitsy might be anywhere on the planet."

As soon as Mrs. DeVine left the club-house, Nancy turned to Bree. "Hold up your hand. We have to take a solemn oath.

We have to promise we'll always stay best friends."

Bree raised her hand. "Yes, we'll never lose touch, even if you are living on the North Pole and I end up at the South Pole."

Then, just to be doubly sure, they pinkie locked on it.

CHAPTER 4

ESTATE
SALE

"Take the next left," Nancy's mom told her dad.

Nancy was excited. They were going to an estate sale. Estates were like mansions—big and fancy—so the furniture for sale was sure to be fancy too. Nancy needed a desk. Up until now she had to do all her homework on her old play table, which was moving into JoJo's room. As a third grader, Nancy required something more grown up, with drawers for her pens and pencils, a place for her schoolbooks, and room for a laptop computer. . . . That is, for whenever she got a laptop computer.

"Maybe we'll find a rare and valuable antique," Nancy said. She was holding her nose, so when she spoke, it sounded as if she had a cold. Last week, driving to Grandpa's, JoJo had regurgitated all over the backseat. It still smelled a little of throw-up.

"An antique? Sure. As long as it costs less than twenty-five dollars," Nancy's mom said.

"My tummy feels funny," JoJo whined.

Nancy's mom swiveled around. "Hold tight, honey! We're almost there."

A moment later the Clancys' car pulled up near a house where several other cars were parked. On the front lawn were some old beach chairs and umbrellas as well as a plastic sandbox with no sand in it. A sign on a tree said, *Estate Sale 9–12 Saturday*.

The house looked a lot like Nancy's, only not as nice. It was painted a funny gray color that reminded Nancy of chewed gum. "If you ask me, that sign is false advertising," Nancy said, disappointed. "This is no estate. This is just an ordinary tag sale."

"I don't know. I'm getting good vibes," her dad said, rubbing his hands together as they walked in the front door.

"Remember, Doug. We're here to get a desk for Nancy. Nothing else."

Nancy's dad couldn't resist buying goofy stuff at tag sales, like the cracked Smurfette mug that he found a couple of weeks ago. "Only twenty cents—can you believe it?" he'd said.

Unfortunately her dad's vibes didn't mean anything. There was no desk for sale, and after Nancy's mom dragged him away from a stack of old *MAD* magazines, they returned to the car and moved on to the next tag sale on her mom's list. No luck there, either, but at the third stop, in an upstairs bedroom of the house, Nancy came upon a small wooden desk with a top that rolled up and down. Although there were lots of scratches on the wood, the desk had a row of little drawers inside as well as cubbyholes. "That's where I could keep letters and other important correspondence," Nancy said.

Her mom had JoJo by the hand. "Doug, jiggle the desk to make sure the legs are

sturdy." Then she turned to Nancy. "So? What do you think?"

"Can we repaint it?" Nancy asked.

"Sure."

"The price is right," Dad said, looking at the tag. "Twenty bucks."

"Oh, I can do way better than that." Nancy's mom suddenly had a gleam in her eyes. She marched downstairs to find the lady who owned the house. Nancy, her dad, and JoJo followed behind.

"Your mother has turned bargaining into an art form," her dad said. "Watch her closely, Nancy. Learn from a pro."

Sure enough, after Mom mentioned the scratches on the desk and brought up the fact that one of the legs wobbled and a knob was missing from a drawer, the price for the desk came down to five dollars. While her mom was bargaining, Nancy browsed through a box of old books and magazines. She found two Nancy Drew mysteries that she hadn't read yet and a picture book on pirates for JoJo.

"Could we get these too, Mom?" Nancy asked. "Please!"

The final bill for everything totaled fifteen dollars, counting the books and a tiny plastic pinball game that Dad had somehow laid his hands on when her mother wasn't looking. He carried the desk to their car.

"I hope you enjoy the desk," the lady said to Nancy. "My daughter used it for years. She was a very good student. You look like a good student too."

"I try my best to be diligent," Nancy said modestly. She figured the lady would know that diligent meant hardworking. "Is the desk an antique?" Nancy asked hopefully.

The lady laughed. "It's old, but I'm

afraid I'm the only antique here."

Then the Clancys all piled into the car and made it home without JoJo regurgitating.

CHAPTER 5

THE SECRET COMPARTMENT

"**B**efore we start painting, pull out all the drawers," Dad told Nancy.

The desk was standing on top of sheets of old newspaper that Nancy had spread out on the floor of the garage. The putty that her dad had put on the bottom of one leg had already hardened, so now

37

the desk didn't wobble.

"It's going to look so gorgeous once we're done!" Nancy said happily. On the way home they'd stopped at the hardware store. Nancy picked out a large can of paint in a fancy shade of white called "alabaster" and a much smaller can of gold paint for the trim.

"Oh, look at this, Dad," Nancy said after she pulled open the end drawer. A small silver key was inside. "I wonder what it opens."

A moment later when she pulled out the next drawer, Nancy thought she might have the answer.

At the very back of the drawer was a small keyhole. That certainly was an odd place for a keyhole to be. Just as that thought crossed her mind, Nancy noticed that this drawer, the one with the keyhole, wasn't as deep as the other.

Suddenly an icy little shiver wiggled through her. She held up the silver key to the keyhole. *Oui, oui, oui!* It was the same size.

"Dad!" Nancy gasped. "I think my desk has a secret compartment!" Just uttering the words "secret compartment" sent another bigger, icier shiver through her. This was like something straight out of a Nancy Drew mystery. Who knew what might be inside? A hidden jewel. A treasure map. A—

"What are you waiting for? Open it!"

With trembling fingers Nancy inserted the key. At least, she tried to.

Although it seemed to fit, the key wouldn't turn.

"Here. You try it, Daddy."

As soon as she handed over the key, her father said, "I see the problem. The tip is bent a little." He scratched his chin. "I know I have a small saw somewhere in here. I could try cutting out the front so you could see what's behind the keyhole."

"No!" Nancy yelped. She didn't want the drawer sawed open. That would wreck her desk before it even got into her room. Also, it seemed against the rules. If you were lucky enough to discover a secret compartment, it should be opened the proper way: with a key. Nancy was almost 100 percent positive that's what Nancy Drew would say.

Dad turned the key over in his hand. "I guess I could try hammering it. Maybe that would straighten it out."

"Yes, please, Daddy. Try that."

While her father hunted for the hammer, Nancy raced over to Bree's house.

Ooh la la! Bree was in her backyard

jumping rope.

"Seventy-one, seventy-two," she counted, gasping for breath. "Stop! Stop! Come with me, *tout de suite.*" Nancy said it like this: "toot sweet." It was French for right now.

"Can't," Bree huffed. "Seventy-eight, seventy-nine . . ." At eighty-one, Bree tripped, and the jump rope went flying from her hands. "Thanks a bunch, Nancy. I was going for my personal best until you messed me up."

"Sorry! But this is important."

The minute Bree heard the mysterious words "secret compartment," she stopped being annoyed and scooted back to the garage with Nancy.

"I did my best," Nancy's dad informed her. "The key is still a little bent."

After Nancy showed Bree the special drawer, she took the key from her father and tried turning it gently in the keyhole. The lock seemed to give a little, so she pressed down on the key harder and pulled.

All at once, the door of the secret compartment swung open.

Nancy and Bree peered inside.

"So, tell me. Tell me. What's in there?" her father said. "I can't stand the suspense!"

ANOTHER
SILVER KEY

here was no jewelry. No treasure map, either. The only thing inside the secret compartment was . . . another key. Another silver key, although this one was bigger and fancier.

Nancy couldn't help feeling let down, although she said to Bree, "It must be important if somebody bothered hiding it in a secret compartment."

"Maybe something in one of the other drawers explains what it's for."

But the other drawers were all empty, which really didn't surprise Nancy. After she put the key back in the secret compartment, she turned to Bree. "So? Want to help me paint?"

Of course Bree did. Besides sleuthing, she and Nancy both loved to do interior decorating. That was the professional term for making your room look prettier.

"Nice job, girls!" her mom said when they were finished applying the alabaster paint.

"With the gold, it's going to look so elegant," Bree said.

"Better wait for the white paint to dry," Nancy's mom advised.

While she was pulling off her smock, Nancy heard someone shouting to them.

"Hey! What are you guys doing?"

It was Grace. Nancy resisted the urge to look at Bree and make a face.

Grace pulled down the kickstand on her bike, a bike that was made in France and cost a fortune, according to Grace.

She already had her helmet off and was walking over to the garage.

"It's my new desk. We're painting it."

"It doesn't look new. It looks old."

"It's new to me," Nancy told Grace. "And it's practically an antique."

"It has a secret compartment with a key!" Bree added.

Nancy had wanted to deliver that exciting bit of news herself. Still, it was very satisfying to hear Grace whistle and say, "No kidding!"

Proudly Nancy pointed at the special drawer that was drying on newspaper. "Don't touch it. The paint's wet. But you can see the little door inside."

Grace bent down and whistled again. "So what was inside?"

"Another key," Nancy said.

"What does it open?"

"We haven't got a clue," Nancy admitted.

"Where'd you get the desk?"

After Grace heard about the tag sale, she said, "So, duh! Just go back there and ask whoever used to own the desk what the key is for."

Nancy and Bree turned to each other and scowled. Grace was right. Why hadn't they thought of that themselves? That worried Nancy. Maybe because it had been so long since their last mystery, their sleuthing skills were getting rusty!

CHAPTER 7

INTERROGATION

At lunch on Monday, Nancy and Bree sat at their usual table under the poster of the five food groups. Nancy had brought the silver key. She held it out for her friends to see while telling the story of how she found it.

Bree passed around a bag of veggie

51

chips and said, "After school, we're going to bike over to the tag-sale house and ask the lady if she knows what the key is for."

"I get to come too," Grace said, appearing out of nowhere. She plopped down her tray and squeezed in next to Clara. "It was my idea, after all."

Nancy grit her teeth. Grace's eavesdropping skills were superb, Nancy had to admit. Grace always heard exactly what you didn't want her to.

"It was *my* idea," Grace repeated as she unwrapped her sandwich. "So it's only fair."

"Okay. On one condition: We ask all the questions," Nancy said. "You can't do any interrogating."

Once they had their helmets on, Nancy and Bree slipped on their trench coats. Nancy's was hot pink. Bree's was purple.

"It's hot. What do you need coats for?" Grace said.

"It so happens that these are the kind of coats detectives wear when they are sleuthing," Nancy informed Grace.

"Whatever," Grace said, and hopped on her made-in-France bike.

It was easy finding the way from school to the lady's house because she lived only two blocks over. After parking their bikes on her front lawn, Nancy knocked at the door. When the lady opened it, Nancy cleared her throat. Then, since she didn't know the lady's name, she smiled and said politely, "Madam, I hope we are not

disturbing you. We need only a few minutes of your time."

"Oh, I remember you." The lady smiled
back. "Your family came to the tag sale.
You bought the rolltop desk." Suddenly
she looked puzzled. "Is something wrong
with it?"

"Oh, no! It's painted alabaster white
now with gold trim and looks great."

"Well, what can I do for you girls?"

"We are trying to solve a mystery," Bree began.

Nancy dug in her trench coat pocket and showed the key to the lady. "This was in a hidden compartment in one of the desk drawers. I'm hoping you know what secret the key will reveal." "Reveal" was also one of Nancy's favorite words. It sounded so much more mysterious than "show."

The lady squinted at the key. "I have no earthly idea. Maybe my daughter knows. It used to be her desk. Would you like me to call her?"

"Thanks! That would be superb!" Nancy said.

The lady left them standing by the door. In less than five minutes she returned. "I'm afraid my daughter was no help either. All she said was that the key had always been there."

"Hmmmm." You couldn't even really count this as new information. Still, Nancy tried mulling over the lady's words.

"Well, was it—" Grace started to speak. But Nancy turned and looked at her sharply.

"Remember the rules."

Then suddenly Nancy thought of a question to ask. "Was the desk brand-new when you got it?"

"Rats. That was my question."

Nancy ignored Grace and was pleased when the lady replied, "No. The desk used to belong to our next-door neighbors."

Ooh la la! Now the investigation was getting somewhere! "The house with the green shutters?" Nancy asked, pointing.

The lady nodded.

"Easy-peasy!" Bree exclaimed. "Let's go!"

"Oh, no, honey. The La Salles moved years ago. In fact, two different families have lived in that house since then."

"Where does the La Salle family live now?" Nancy took out her sleuthing notebook and pen.

"The last I heard, they were in New York City."

The Big Apple! How glamorous, although New York City was way too far away to bike to. "Do you have their phone number or an email address?"

"I did. But I don't know if either one is current. We haven't been in touch for years. And . . ." The lady paused for a second.

"Well, I'm sorry, but I really wouldn't be comfortable giving out that kind of information." The lady backed away from the front door. It was clear that she didn't want to be interrogated anymore. Suddenly Nancy started feeling more like a pest than a practically professional sleuth.

"We're sorry to have bothered you. And we thank you for your time," Nancy said sadly.

"Good luck!" the lady said.

Nancy and Bree turned to leave, but Grace butted in.

"Listen, if you do find an email address or something," she said to the lady, "you could write and see if your old neighbors would let us email them."

"Yesss." The lady drew out the word as if she were considering it. "I suppose I could do that."

"My name is Nancy, and this is my family's email address." Nancy wrote down clancyfamily@arrow.com and handed the slip of paper to the lady.

"Thanks so much," Nancy said, and pocketed her notepad. Then the three girls hopped back on their bikes and rode home. Nancy wasn't completely convinced the lady really would bother to try to track down her old neighbors. And Nancy certainly didn't like the way Grace had said "us" before, as if she were a part of the investigation. However, Nancy had to hand it to Grace. If not for her, their sleuthing would have come to a dead end. Sometimes it really paid off to be a pest!

CHAPTER 8

A BREAK IN THE CASE

Later that night, while Nancy was searching for something superb to put in the class time capsule, she heard her dad calling.

"Nancy, there's an email for you . . . at least I think it's for you. Do you know someone named Ann Tyler?"

Nancy zipped downstairs to the living room, where her father sat with his laptop computer.

"Let me see, Dad!" Nancy peered over her dad's shoulder at the screen.

Oui, oui, oui! The email was from the tag-sale lady! Nancy read it out loud.

To: clancyfamily@arrow.com

Hello, Nancy,

You are in luck. Here is the email address for Diana La Salle. I wrote her and it is fine for you to contact her daughter, Olivia, who owned the desk. Here is Olivia's phone number. I hope you are able to solve the mystery.

Sincerely yours,

Ann Tyler

Diana La Salle! Olivia La Salle. In her entire life, Nancy had never heard such elegant names. They sounded characters in a Nancy Drew book. Nice ones. Not evil ones. Nancy kept repeating the phone number aloud as she ran toward the kitchen to make the call.

"Hold on, Sherlock," her dad said. "What's going on here? What mystery?"

Nancy's mother and JoJo were sitting on the sofa with the tag-sale book on pirates. Her mother stopped reading. Now both her parents were looking at Nancy, waiting for an answer.

"It's kind of complicated," Nancy began.

Her mom and dad were not at all pleased when they heard she had biked over to a stranger's house.

"She isn't a stranger. We all were at her house for the tag sale!"

"That doesn't make her a close personal friend," her dad pointed out.

"But we didn't go inside. We just stood at the door."

After Nancy had apologized many times, she asked, "So? Will you let me call now? Please?"

Her parents relented, which was the grown-up way of saying they gave in.

"*Merci. Merci beaucoup* with sugar on top!" Nancy blew kisses at them. Then she thought of something. "Ooh, I have to inform Bree of this."

Upstairs in her room, Nancy sent off a message in their Top-Secret Special Delivery mailbox. It hung from a long rope strung in between their bedroom windows. Nancy rang the bell, which meant mail was coming.

There's been a break in the case! her note read. *Can you come over* tout de suite?

Bree arrived in a flash. Nancy had Olivia La Salle's number written down. She punched it in and held the receiver between them so they both could listen. What they learned was music to their ears. Not only had the desk belonged to Olivia La Salle, but she was quite sure she knew what the silver key opened. "If you'd like to come over, I can show you," she offered.

After Nancy and Bree hung up, they jumped up and down and then high-fived

each other. Fortunately, Olivia La Salle no longer lived in Gotham, which was another name for New York City. She lived in a town that was fifteen minutes away by car.

Unfortunately, neither of Nancy's parents could spare the time to drive there until the weekend. Though only a few days away, the weekend seemed impossibly far into the future. No way could Nancy and Bree wait that long.

"Let me see what I can do!" Bree said, and sped back to her house.

Nancy waited in her room for the bell to ring. When it did, she reeled in the rope and opened the note in the basket.

Chérie, *my dad will take us tomorrow after school!*

Nancy opened the secret compartment and gazed at the silver key. Soon its secret would be revealed. Knowing that made her shiver with pleasure.

CHAPTER 9

THE TIME CAPSULE

The next day, Grace was absent, which solved the problem of whether to invite her sleuthing. Many kids came in with stuff for the time capsule, which was a big box from Sibley's department store. Lionel brought in a whoopee cushion. Bree had

a long printed-out bill from a supermarket register. She said, "Kids of the future can see what milk and ice cream and cereal and lots of other food used to cost."

Bree beamed when Mr. D said, "What a superb idea."

Joel, who wanted to be an astronaut, had a Lego rocket ship. Clara brought in very shiny coins, a penny, a nickel, and a dime.

"Won't there still be money fifty years from now?" Tamar wanted to know.

Mr. D wasn't sure. "By then every-body might be using plastic money cards instead of real money."

"My coins were made this year." Clara showed the class where the date was on each. "So in fifty years, they'll be exactly fifty years old."

In the afternoon, during creative writing, Nancy continued the latest exploits—which were adventures but more exciting—of Lucette Fromage. She was a nine-year-old girl Nancy had made up.

This time, Nancy decided to have Lucette Fromage magically travel back in time to Paris, France, hundreds of years ago.

Nancy began writing. "Lucette found herself in a castle garden where a beautiful lady said *"Bonjour"* to her. She was dressed in a *très*-fancy gown and carried a lace parasol. Although the lady was young, her hair was white. That was because she was wearing a big, powdered wig.

"Tout de suite Lucette realized this lady was the queen of France."

Nancy put down her pencil and thought about what should come next. Last week she had read a book about this queen. Her name was Marie. The queen loved jewels and eating cake. But she didn't care about the poor people of Paris, France. Nancy began writing again.

"Lucette curtsied and said, 'Your Majesty, I come from the future and I am here to warn you. You must act nicer to peasant-folk or they will do something terrible to you!"

Even writing fast, the last bell rang before Nancy had finished her story. She grabbed her backpack and she and Bree were outside the school building in record time.

CHAPTER 10

A DEAD END

"**H**i, Pop!" Bree shouted, waving. Her father waved back from inside the first car in a long line that snaked down the block.

As soon as they were buckled into their seat belts, off they went to visit Olivia La Salle.

Bree's dad had GPS in his car, so driving to Olivia La Salle's house was a cinch.

Nancy loved listening to the sophisticated voice of the GPS lady, who announced in practically no time, "You have arrived at your destination."

Ooh la la! The house was a genuine McMansion. It was brand-new and big—really big—with the kind of tower that Nancy knew was called a turret. Castles often came with turrets.

Olivia La Salle greeted them at the door. Double ooh la la. She was glamorous. Her wavy red hair looked as if she had just left a beauty salon. Her makeup was applied perfectly. When she smiled, both her top and bottom teeth showed. "So who's the proud new owner of my desk?"

"I am. I'm Nancy Clancy, and this is my best friend, Bree, and her dad, Mr.

Sylvester James."

"Well, I think it was very enterprising of you girls to track me down," she said cheerily, and motioned everyone inside. "We'll go in the family room and you can see what your key opens."

As soon as they walked into the front hall, Bree's dad snapped his fingers. "It just hit me." He shook his head and chuckled. "I knew you looked familiar, and now I recognize the voice—you're on Channel Three News."

Olivia La Salle laughed merrily. "Guilty as charged." She spread both arms out. "Olivia La Salle—your Channel Three Weather Gal."

Nancy, who was following bchind the grown-ups, couldn't help letting out a gasp. She turned to Bree. She looked equally stunned.

This was almost too good to be true. Not only did Nancy's desk come with a mystery, it used to belong to a celebrity! A television personality!

They were shown into a room with the largest flat-screen TV Nancy had ever seen.

"So, ladies, shall we get down to business?" Olivia La Salle said. While she searched through a cabinet, Nancy took the silver key from her pocket. What would it unlock? Probably something important from Olivia La Salle's past. Maybe a keepsake box with memories of her first sweetheart—stuff like dead flowers, photos, and love letters. Or a diary that Olivia La Salle had kept when she was a young girl with big dreams of becoming a Weather Gal.

Olivia La Salle turned. She was holding a jewelry box. It was pink fake leather with a gold design around the rim. Nancy had

one just like it. It was a birthday present from her grandma.

"So open it! What are you waiting for?" Olivia La Salle laughed her merry laugh again. But then she took a closer look at the key in Nancy's hand. Everyone could see it was much too big to fit into the tiny lock on the jewelry box. "Aw, gee. And I was so sure I had stashed the key in the desk you have now—to keep my jewelry safe from my sister."

"In the desk drawer with the secret compartment?" Nancy asked.

"Secret compartment? No, I never knew about any secret compartment." When the lady shook her head, her hairdo didn't move. "Gee, I'm sorry. You came all the way over here, and I haven't been any help solving your mystery." Then the lady made a goofy face with her lower lip pooched out, like a baby about to cry.

Bree's dad laughed. "That's the face you make on TV when bad weather's coming!"

"At least let me show you what happens when the jewelry box is opened. It's so cute. All I need is a paper clip." She went over to a big desk in the corner.

Nancy and Bree both knew what they'd see. Still, they pretended to act

surprised when a little plastic ballerina popped up from the top tray. The
little ballerina twirled around to the same
music as Nancy's did.

"That's very enchanting," Nancy said to
be polite. "Enchanting" was a more interesting word than "lovely."

Five minutes later, the GPS lady was

directing them home. Sad to say, the mystery had reached a dead end. Still, meeting a genuine celebrity wasn't something that happened every day. Before they left, Olivia La Salle had presented both Nancy and Bree with a photograph of herself. She had written, *Here's to blue skies! From Olivia La Salle, your Channel 3 Weather Gal.*

CHAPTER 11

MORE SLEUTHING

Nancy was writing at her alabaster-white desk. Her story about Lucette Fromage was almost finished. Nancy was 100 percent positive that writing at a desk rather than at a play table gave her more inspired ideas.

At this point Nancy had to decide whether Lucette would reveal to the queen of France that she was going to get her head chopped off! Perhaps it would make a better story if Queen Marie wasn't told and decided, all on her own, to be kinder to the poor people of France. Yes! That was how Nancy would end it.

Done and done! Nancy put her story in her backpack. But mystery was kind of like a mosquito bite. It was hard not to keep scratching it. The photo of Olivia La Salle was now taped on the wall right above Nancy's desk.

The Weather Gal had not revealed the secret to the silver key. But maybe the problem was that Nancy and Bree had not asked enough questions.

Suddenly Nancy wished she could snap her fingers the way Bree's dad could, because something occurred to her. They hadn't asked Olivia La Salle a very basic question.

Nancy scooted over to Bree's house. Maybe they hadn't hit a dead end after all.

A message on Olivia La Salle's telephone:

"Hello, Ms. La Salle. It's Nancy and Bree. We forgot one thing to ask you. Would you please call this number at your earliest convenience? Thank you."

"I didn't expect her to be home," Bree said, glancing at the clock on her desk. "She's probably at the TV station, getting ready for the weather report. The news goes on in half an hour."

"You're right." Nancy blew through her lips and fell back on Bree's bed. "It'll be ages before she calls back . . . if she even bothers to."

Waiting was one of Nancy's absolute least-favorite things to do.

"I know!" Nancy sat up. "Let's call her at the TV station."

Bree scrunched up her nose. She was more patient than Nancy was. But not by

much. She looked over at her photo of Olivia La Salle. It was already in a frame on her bedside table. "What if she starts thinking we're pests?"

"She won't. Remember how she said we were enterprising to track her down?" Then Nancy reminded Bree that a good sleuth needed to be persistent. That meant being stubborn, but in a good way.

"That's true," Bree said, considering Nancy's point. "Okay! Let's do it!"

The telephone book was in the kitchen. It was decided that Bree would make the call because her voice sounded more mature than Nancy's. They held the phone between them while Bree punched in the number.

"Good evening. This is WJIM. How may I help you?" a voice said. It sounded a lot like the voice of the GPS lady.

Bree squeezed Nancy's hand hard. "Hello. May I please speak to Olivia La

Salle, the Weather Gal?"

There was a pause on the other end of the line. "Who is calling, please?"

"My name is Bree James."

"Ms. La Salle is in makeup now. Is she expecting your call?"

"Not exactly. My friend and I visited her yesterday. Please, it'll only take a second."

Another pause.

"Hold on while I see if she is available."

With their free hands, both Nancy and Bree crossed their fingers.

It was only a moment later before they heard the jolly voice of Olivia La Salle asking, "Hi there. What's up?"

"Ms. La Salle, we forgot to ask something."

"Fire away, Bree."

"Was the desk brand-new when you got it?"

"No, it wasn't. It used to belong to my aunt Elizabeth."

Ooh la la! The trail was no longer at a dead end!

"Would your aunt mind if we got in touch with her?" Bree asked.

It took just a minute for Olivia La Salle to find her aunt's email address.

Nancy raced to get a pen and paper for Bree.

"My aunt is going to get a real kick out of you girls," Olivia La Salle said, and then before she hung up, she added, "Here's a little weather tip: Wear rain-coats tomorrow!"

CHAPTER 12

A SUPERB
CLUE

The time capsule was filling up. Mr. Dudeny had brought in a campaign button from the last time people voted for president. Nola had a bunch of stamps in an envelope, which she claimed would be worth a bundle of money in fifty years.

Grace brought in stubs from movie tickets and a photo of the shopping mall. "The titles of the movies are on the stubs so kids of the future can see what was popular with kids of the past."

"Hold on! That's us you're talking about! We're not the past. Not yet," Tamar pointed out.

Nancy still hadn't settled on what to add to the time capsule. And tomorrow was the deadline. So far it was between a yellow felt pennant that said *Ada M. Draezel Elementary School* or the 3D class picture, which her parents were not eager to part with. Neither really seemed that special.

At lunch Grace asked in a sarcastic voice, "So how is your little investigation going?"

"Very well, *merci beaucoup,*" Nancy said. Since Grace had been absent yesterday when Bree and Nancy had shown the class their photos of Olivia La Salle, Nancy had the pleasure of repeating the whole story for Grace.

"We're waiting to hear from her aunt Elizabeth now," Bree said.

Grace just kept eating her sandwich and didn't reply.

When Nancy got home that afternoon, her mom said, "You and Bree can expect a visitor in about forty-five minutes." It turned

out that Olivia La Salle's aunt Elizabeth lived in the retirement community downtown.

Nancy and Bree had cookies and lemonade waiting in the clubhouse for their guest, who arrived right on time. A very tall lady, taller even than Nancy's dad, hopped out of a blue sports car.

Nancy figured Aunt Elizabeth would be old. And she was. But Nancy hadn't expected her to be wearing a Beatles T-shirt, neon-green tights, or orange high tops. Her gray hair was pulled back in a ponytail and she had a bag with a rolled-up gym mat slung over her shoulder.

Aunt Elizabeth—who introduced herself

as Miss Simon—explained that she was
on her way to yoga class. "But your message sounded urgent, so here I am."

Urgent? Nancy had never heard that
word before, but she could tell it meant
serious and important.

"Yes. It's most urgent," Nancy agreed.

The girls led Miss Simon to Nancy's room.

"Wow! It certainly looks a lot fancier now," she said upon seeing the desk. She went straight to the drawer with the secret compartment and opened it. "This was the niftiest thing about the desk. It was like something in a Nancy Drew mystery."

"You liked Nancy Drew?" Nancy and Bree both exclaimed.

"Well, of course I did!"

Now came the all-important question. "Do you know what the silver key opens?" Nancy asked.

Miss Simon took the key from the secret compartment and held it her hand. The way she just kept staring at it, not saying a word, began to get a little spooky. Finally she spoke.

"The key doesn't open any-thing."

Say what?! That was definitely not the right answer!

But then Miss Simon continued. "I used to wear this key on a long chain around my neck. My best friend had one exactly like it. We bought them together and swore never to take them off. It meant our friendship would last forever."

"But you did take it off. It was in the drawer," Bree pointed out.

"My family moved to a new town, and after a while I stopped wearing it. The two of us meant to stay best friends, but that didn't happen." Miss Simon shook her head, then shrugged. "Still, the key was important to me, so I kept it in the secret compartment. . . . I haven't seen it in— well, it must be close to fifty years."

There was no time for refreshments because Miss Simon didn't want to be late for her yoga class. Nancy gave her back the silver key and Miss Simon took off in her car, leaving Nancy and Bree in the clubhouse eating cookies and drinking lemonade. They weren't despondent, which was way, way sadder than sad. But they were both very let down.

"At least we solved the mystery," Bree said, sighing. Then she scraped off all the white part of an Oreo with her teeth. "But I wanted a happy, exciting ending."

"Me too," Nancy said. "In a book it would have turned out much better."

After Bree left, Nancy stayed to polish off the last cookie.

Then she stood and dusted off cookie crumbs. That's when she noticed the red spiral-bound album. The one Mrs. DeVine had brought over the other day.

Nancy took it back to her room for safe-keeping. On most Saturdays Nancy and Bree were invited to tea at Mrs. DeVine's. She would return it then.

Sitting cross-legged on her bed, Nancy leafed through the album. Mrs. DeVine, who was Marjorie or Margie back then, had pasted in postcards from places her

family had visited on vacations as well as lots of photos of people Nancy figured were relatives.

On one page was a strip of three photos of Mrs. DeVine and her old best friend, which had been taken in a photo booth. In each photo, the two girls were making goofy faces. Nancy was impressed at how Mrs. DeVine could make her eyes go completely crossed. But that wasn't what caught Nancy's attention. In the last picture the friends were each holding something up to the camera. Nancy swallowed hard. She was pretty sure she could make out what was in their hands, but she wanted to be 100 percent positive. So she got out her magnifying glass, the special one for sleuthing that had rhinestones on it.

Oui, oui, oui! She definitely was seeing what she thought she saw.

She dashed off a message to Bree and sent it off in the mail basket.

Come tout de suite*!* it said.

But Bree didn't show up until after dinner. And she wasn't all that astonished when Nancy held the magnifying glass over the photo.

"See what they're holding, Bree? Keys! Silver keys that are on long chains around their necks!"

"So you think that proves Aunt Elizabeth—I mean, Miss Simon—used to be Mrs. DeVine's best friend?" Bree looked skeptical.

Nancy nodded. "I'm almost positive." Actually she wasn't, but she wanted it to be true.

Bree was shaking her head. "You can't even tell if the keys are silver. The pictures are in black-and-white."

"That's true. But you can't tell that they *aren't* silver."

"I know how to get to the bottom of this," Bree said.

They went downstairs to use the computer. Bree fired off an email to Miss Simon. All it said was, *We forgot to ask something. When you were a kid, did you have a nickname?*

Later that evening, Nancy was reading

one of her new Nancy Drew books when her mom looked up from the computer and said, "Sweetie, there's an email for you."

The moment Nancy finished reading it, she started screaming and hopping up and down.

"Did we just win the lottery?" her dad asked.

Nancy didn't answer. She was already half-way up the stairs.

This is what her message to Bree said:

Chérie. *Miss Simon had a nickname! It was Bitsy!!!!!!!!!!!!*

CHAPTER 13

MYSTERY SOLVED

"**Y**ou're putting a friendship bracelet in the time capsule?" Grace looked at Nancy and rolled her eyes. "That's dumb."

Mr. Dudeny heard her. "Grace, remember how you and I have talked—several times—about treating classmates with respect?"

Grace didn't answer. Mr. D stood staring at her, waiting.

Finally Grace said, "Sorry, Nancy."

Nancy didn't care whether Grace thought the friendship bracelet was dumb. Attached to it were instructions for making a friendship bracelet, in case kids of the future didn't know how, as well as a photo of Bree and herself. On the back she had written the date, their names, and the words "Best friends forever." When the time capsule would be opened, she and Bree would be old ladies, as old as Mrs. DeVine and—Nancy stopped, because she could feel her brain getting all twisted up in that weird way again.

At lunch Nancy and Bree explained to their friends how they had solved the secret of the silver key and what they were planning for Saturday.

Dear Mrs. DeVine:
You are invited to Cohen's Ice Cream Shoppe, Saturday at three o'clock. It's our treat.
Love,
Nancy and Bree

CHAPTER 14

REUNION

"I must say, you girls are acting awfully mysterious," Mrs. DeVine said as they took their seats in a booth at Cohen's Ice Cream Shoppe.

Nancy and Bree giggled but didn't answer. Nancy was so excited she couldn't sit still. Neither could Bree. She was squirming around as if she had ants in her pants.

It was 2:58, according to the giant clock that had hands in the shape of ice cream cones. Nancy pretended to look at the menu when actually her eyes were trained on the front door.

At 3:01, Aunt Elizabeth or Miss Simon or Bitsy, as she used to be called, walked in.

"Over here!" Bree stood up, waving.

Miss Simon smiled and headed for their booth. Then all of a sudden she stopped and blinked. Her hand flew to her

mouth. Nancy looked across the table at Mrs. DeVine. She had the same startled expression. Her hand was pressed against her chest.

"No! It can't be!" Mrs. DeVine cried. Her eyes were open as wide as a doll's. "Bitsy?"

"Margie?"

Nancy and Bree bounced in their seats triumphantly as Mrs. DeVine rose with her arms outstretched.

Oui! Oui! Oui! Nancy and Bree had pulled it off. A surprise reunion!

The old friends hugged and kissed and cried a little.

"Oh, look. I got lipstick smeared all over you!" Mrs. DeVine said, sitting down. She took a napkin from the dispenser and began rubbing Miss Simon's cheek.

"And your mascara is running! You have raccoon eyes!" Miss Simon said.

Then they turned to each other and hugged and kissed and cried some more.

When the ladies finally settled down, Mrs. DeVine asked Nancy and Bree, "How on earth did you find Bitsy?"

So they went through the whole story, step by step. "It all started with a silver key that I found in my desk."

"Your desk? What was it doing there?" Mrs. DeVine looked puzzled.

"The desk used to belong to Miss Simon. It wound up at a tag sale. That's where Nancy got it," Bree explained.

"Your rolltop desk?" Mrs. DeVine asked Miss Simon. Then she addressed Nancy and Bree. "Oh, was I jealous. *My* desk didn't have a secret compartment."

"Do you still have yours?" Miss Simon wanted to know. "The silver key, I mean?"

"Oh yes!" Mrs. DeVine replied. "In my jewelry box."

It turned out that the ladies now lived only ten minutes away from each other.

"I was living in Mexico for years, but the hot weather got to be too much for me," Miss Simon explained. "So I moved back here of all places. To the Geezers' Palace."

Mrs. DeVine laughed. "I assume you are talking about Elwood Retirement Community."

Right away the ladies began updating each other on the facts of their lives.

Bitsy had never married—"too much trouble," she said—and had lived all over the world. She used to be a journalist, which Nancy knew was the professional name for a reporter.

Mrs. DeVine told Bitsy about the beauty salon that she had owned. Its name was Hair and Now. Nancy and Bree already

knew that. But they hadn't realized that their neighbor had been married three times!

"I have three children, one from each husband. But no grandchildren, not yet." Mrs. DeVine pointed at Nancy and Bree. "They're my substitute granddaughters."

A waiter appeared with menus for

everyone and said, "I'll be back in a minute to take your orders, ladies."

"No, wait. Do you girls know what you want?" Miss Simon asked Nancy and Bree.

"We'll each have the Death by Chocolate, please," Nancy said. Whenever they came to Cohen's, that was always what they ordered. It came with two scoops of chocolate ice cream on a giant brownie in a pool of hot-fudge sauce, topped with chocolate-flavored whipped cream. Heaven!

"And you, ma'am, what would you like?" the waiter asked

Mrs. DeVine. Mrs. DeVine was about to order but Miss Simon interrupted. "Margie here will have coffee ice cream with butterscotch sauce and slivered almonds, please."

"That's absolutely correct," Mrs. DeVine said. "And Bitsy here would like two scoops of strawberry ice cream with sprinkles— the multicolored ones—and a mountain of whipped cream."

Both ladies marveled over how they still remembered what ice cream the other one liked. But that didn't strike Nancy as surprising. Of course your best friend would know all the important stuff about you!

Their orders arrived, and as usual Nancy had to help Bree finish off the last part of her brownie. The ladies were busy exchanging phone numbers and email addresses. By the time everyone was ready to leave, they had made dinner plans for the following Tuesday. And they were both going to wear their silver keys on a chain around their necks—just like they used to.

At the parking lot behind Cohen's, Miss Simon pulled out her car keys and was heading for her car, when Nancy whispered something to Bree.

"We want both of you to take a solemn oath," Nancy said.

"That's right." Bree nodded. "You have to promise to stay friends this time—forever."

After raising their right hands, the ladies repeated Bree's words.

Then, just to be doubly sure, Nancy made them pinkie lock on it!

A CHAPTER BOOK SERIES STARRING EVERYONE'S FAVORITE FANCY GIRL

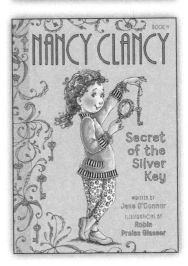

HARPER
An Imprint of HarperCollinsPublishers

www.fancynancyworld.com